B53 025 907 2

KT-144-976

This Little Tiger book belongs to:

_____

_____

_____

For Jack and Joe Mongredien,

and their very special Grandpa – S M

For Anne and Paul, with love – C B

ROTHERHAM LIBRARY
SERVICE

B53025907

| Bertrams | 10/08/2012 |
|----------|------------|
| JF | £5.99 |
| KIP | |

LITTLE TIGER PRESS

An imprint of Magi Publications
1 The Coda Centre, 189 Munster Road, London SW6 6AW
www.littletigerpress.com

First published in Great Britain 2011
This edition published 2012

Text copyright © Sue Mongredien 2011
Illustrations copyright © Cee Biscoe 2011

Sue Mongredien and Cee Biscoe have asserted their rights
to be identified as the author and illustrator of this work under
the Copyright, Designs and Patents Act, 1988

A CIP catalogue record for this book is available
from the British Library

All rights reserved • ISBN 978-1-84895-234-8

Printed in China • LTP/1400/0387/0312

2 4 6 8 10 9 7 5 3

# Before We Go To Bed

Sue
Mongredien

Cee
Biscoe

LITTLE TIGER PRESS
London

Barney and Grandpa Bear were tramping
home together after a busy day.
  "What are we going to do next?"
Barney asked.
  "Next?" chuckled Grandpa in surprise.
"Next, I think it's bedtime, Barney!"

Grandpa pulled off Barney's boots with a heave-squelch-plop! "Now, let's get you ready for bed," he said.

"Not yet, Grandpa!" Barney cried. "I ALWAYS have a GIANT bowl of porridge before I go to bed. Yummy, scrummy porridge, with sticky, licky honey!"
"Are you sure?" asked Grandpa.

"Oh yes," said Barney.
"Come on!"

Barney showed Grandpa what a brilliant porridge-maker he was.

"And now for the honey!" he cheered. But the honey was runny . . . and it went EVERYWHERE.

"Whoops-a-daisy!" giggled Barney.

"Time for bed now," said Grandpa,
when Barney's tummy was full.

"But I ALWAYS have a big, bubbly bath before
I go to bed!" said Barney. "A splishy-sloshy
bath with my squeezy-squirty toys."

"I suppose you are a rather sticky bear," Grandpa said, as Barney tipped in ALL the bubble bath with a glug-glug-gloop.

Barney splished and sploshed in his lovely, bubbly bath. The water went EVERYWHERE.

"Whoops-a-daisy!" giggled Barney.

"All clean!" Grandpa said. "It MUST be bedtime now."

"But I'll NEVER get to sleep without a story," Barney said. "A spooky, scare-a-bear story with horrible, hairy monsters."

"Is a spooky, scare-a-bear story a good idea before bed?" Grandpa wondered.

"Don't worry, Grandpa," said Barney. "It's only a story. It's not real."

So Grandpa read the story.

Afterwards, Grandpa put the light
on again to make them both feel better.

"Maybe we shouldn't go to sleep just yet," he said.

"I've got a brilliant idea," said Barney.
"We could bounce on the bed! Shall we, Grandpa?"

Grandpa smiled.
"All right then," he said.
First they did little bear bounces.

Next they did bigger
bear bounces.

And then they did
**great big,**
**springy-zingy,**
**boingy-bear**
**bounces!**

Until...

Crash! went the bed.

"Whoops-a-daisy!"
went Barney and Grandpa.

"Sounds to me like it's definitely bedtime,"
said Grandpa, tucking Barney under
the covers.

"There's just one more thing I need,"
said Barney sleepily. "A super-squeezy,
squishy-squashy . . ."

# "…BEAR HUG!"

Then both bears fell fast asleep
until morning.

# More Little Tiger books to read before you go to bed!

Star Friends
Tracey Corderoy
Alison Edgson

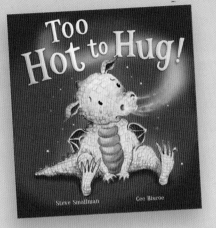

Too Hot to Hug!
Steve Smallman
Cee Biscoe

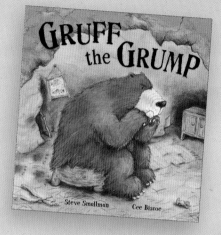

GRUFF the GRUMP
Steve Smallman
Cee Biscoe

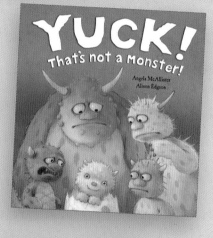

YUCK! That's not a monster!
Angela McAllister
Alison Edgson

The Bears in the Bed and the Great Big Storm
Paul Bright
Jane Chapman

Bedtime Little Ones!

For information regarding any of the above titles
or for our catalogue, please contact us:
Little Tiger Press, 1 The Coda Centre,
189 Munster Road, London SW6 6AW
Tel: 020 7385 6333 • Fax: 020 7385 7333
E-mail: info@littletiger.co.uk • www.littletigerpress.com